GANDERS

JENNIFER ZABEL

Wimbleball

illustrated by
Robert Geary

HODDER AND STOUGHTON
London Sydney Auckland Toronto

British Library Cataloguing in Publication Data

Zabel, Jennifer
   Wimbleball.
   I. Title
   823.914 [J]

   ISBN 0–240–51428–0

Text copyright © Jennifer Zabel 1990
Illustrations copyright © Hodder and Stoughton Ltd 1990

First published 1990

Published by Hodder and Stoughton Children's Books,
a division of Hodder and Stoughton Ltd,
Mill Road, Dunton Green, Sevenoaks, Kent TN13 2YA

Photoset by En to En, Tunbridge Wells, Kent

Printed in Great Britain by T. J. Press (Padstow) Ltd,
Padstow, Cornwall

1 A Cottage for Sale

Wimbleball was a cat. He lived in Kipper
Cottage with Frank Fingle, the fisherman.
If you fell off the wall at the bottom of their
backyard, you ended up in the River Wisk.
Wimbleball had fallen off once. He was
having a fight with Turpin the tomcat at the
time. But Turpin had fallen off, too, and got
a lot wetter than Wimbleball. Or so
Wimbleball said.

At five o'clock every morning Frank and Wimbleball went fishing. Frank's boat was tied to a ring in the harbour wall. You went down some stone steps covered in seaweed to get to it. The boat was called *Bobber,* because it bobbed about a lot. Wimbleball liked sitting on top of the cabin, like a mascot. He never fell off. Not even when there was a storm and *Bobber* bobbed about so much that Frank lost his sandwiches over the side.

When they got back they carried the lobsters and crabs and buckets of fish up the stone steps into the backyard. Then people like Mrs Trundle and Henry came to buy them. Henry was the cook at the Pelican Hotel, and the Pelican Hotel was the best hotel in Penwisk. Mrs Trundle was Mrs Trundle.

One day they got back to find Mrs Trundle already waiting with her fish basket.

'Morning, Mrs Trundle!' called Frank. 'Nice bit of mackerel for you today?'

But Mrs Trundle wasn't interested in a nice bit of mackerel.

'It's for sale!' she cried.

'What's for sale?' asked Frank.

'Crab Cottage!' cried Mrs Trundle. 'They've put a FOR SALE sign up at the front!'

Frank and Wimbleball went round to look. And they had.

Now Crab Cottage was joined on to Kipper Cottage. It had been empty for ages and ages and was full of mice. They squeaked and scuttled all night long.

'No more mice!' said Frank. 'Good!'

No more mice! thought Wimbleball. Rats!
And he stalked back home to Kipper
Cottage, flopped down in his box,
and sulked.

The next day lots of people came to look
at Crab Cottage. A man in a smart suit
showed them round. He showed them
round the backyard, too.

'Morning!' beamed Frank, from his own backyard. He was sitting on his bench in the sunshine mending his nets.

'Oh!' said the man, staring at a cod's head on top of the wall. It was the left-overs from Wimbleball's breakfast.
'Oh dear!'

After that the man in the smart suit stopped showing people round the backyard. They just had a quick peep at it from the bedroom window.

One week later down came the FOR SALE sign and up went a SOLD sign. Frank was delighted. Wimbleball wasn't.

That night he went hunting mice in Crab
Cottage. He'd been doing it every night for
ages and ages. He scrambled in through a
crack at the top of the kitchen window.
He padded across the dusty floorboards
and hid in his favourite corner. He waited.
Sure enough, the silly mice came popping
out of their holes and started washing their
whiskers in the moonlight.

Wham! went Wimbleball's paw.

Now the speed of Wimbleball's paw was
well known to every mouse in Penwisk.
It never missed.

Tonight it missed. By miles. Every mouse
was back in its hole before Wimbleball's
paw hit the floorboards.

'Ow!' went Wimbleball. And he knew
then that things would never ever be the
same again.

2 A New Neighbour

Wimbleball was behind Mrs Trundle's
dustbin, stalking seagulls with Turpin,
when the removal van came. It was so big
it blocked the road. Immediately Mrs
Trundle's door shot open and out she came
with a bucket of water.

'Duck!' hissed Wimbleball.

But Mrs Trundle had only come out to scrub her front step.

Two men got out of the van and started to unload furniture. A lady got out, too. She was rather posh with a poky face and a string of pearls. *Tip-tap-tip-tap* went the heels of her shoes on the cobbles. Then she disappeared into Crab Cottage.

'Oh *very* la-di-da!' said Mrs Trundle, scrubbing away at her front step. 'Very la-di-da *indeed*!'

Wimbleball and Turpin went for a root round the inside of the van. Turpin tried out a blue velvet armchair with his claws.

'Not bad,' he said.

Wimbleball peered down from the top of a wardrobe. There were lots and lots of tables at the back of the van, all piled on top of each other.

'How many tables have you got in your house?' he asked Turpin.

'One,' said Turpin. 'With four legs.'

Just then the men came back. Wimbleball and Turpin dived out of the van and Turpin ran straight home up Pansy Lane for his dinner.

Wimbleball jumped over the wall and in through the back door of Kipper Cottage. *His* dinner wasn't ready yet. Frank hadn't made it. Frank was too busy trimming his beard over the kitchen sink. He'd got his best shirt on, too.

'That's better!' he said at last. 'Now, let's pop round and say hello!'

Two minutes later he was knocking on the back door of Crab Cottage. The lady with the poky face came out. 'Yes?' she said.

'I'm Frank Fingle,' said Frank. 'From next door. I've just popped round to say hello.'

'Well, I'm Miss Tripp!' said Miss Tripp. 'And I *do* hope you're going to do something about that backyard, Mr Fingle!'

'What backyard?' asked Frank.

'*Your* backyard,' said Miss Tripp. 'I can't have the smell of dead cod drifting all over my cream teas, you know!'

'What cream teas?' asked Frank.

'*My* cream teas!' said Miss Tripp.
'I'm turning Crab Cottage into a tea-shop, Mr Fingle, and you can't have a smelly backyard next door to a tea-shop.
The customers wouldn't like it. Good evening!' And *bang* went the door of Crab Cottage.

That night Wimbleball sat on the rug, blinking, as Frank made his bed-time cocoa. Frank was cross.

'Right old crab she is!' he grumbled. 'Just right for Crab Cottage.' And up to bed he stomped with his cocoa and hot-water bottle.

Wimbleball put his nose on his paws. Did cream teas taste nicer than mice, he wondered. After a while he wandered round to Crab Cottage to see if the crack at the top of the kitchen window was still there.

It wasn't.

3 Cream Teas

At five o'clock in the morning Frank and
Wimbleball set off fishing. Everyone was
always fast asleep when Frank and
Wimbleball set off fishing. But not today.
Today Miss Tripp was up painting her tea-
shop and singing her head off at the same
time.

Frank tried to tiptoe past, but Miss Tripp poked her paintbrush at him.

'No more nasty nets hanging around, I hope, Mr Fingle!' she said. 'I'm opening my tea-shop tomorrow!'

Frank stamped down the steps and started *Bobber*'s engine. As loudly as he

could. Wimbleball just had time to spring
on top of the cabin before they were off.
Down the River Wisk and out to the open
sea.

It was a bad day. They caught one crab,
two tiddlers, and a lump of seaweed.

'It's that Miss Tripp's fault!' grumbled
Frank, as they chugged back home. 'She's
scared 'em all off. I wonder what she's up
to now?'

He took his telescope out of his pocket
and peered in the direction of Penwisk.
Miss Tripp was up a ladder hammering a
huge sign to the wall of Crab Cottage.
CREAM TEAS it said, in great big capital
letters.

'You can see that sign a mile off!' Frank told Miss Tripp crossly, as soon as they got back. 'I bet you could see that sign from the Port Coddle road!' The Port Coddle road was on the far side of the River Wisk, and Port Coddle was a holiday town in the next bay.

'Good!' said Miss Tripp. 'Then all the holidaymakers will drive round to Penwisk for a cream tea in my tea-shop.'

Just then Henry, the cook from the Pelican Hotel, arrived with his fish basket. When he saw the sign, his face went as red as a lobster.

'The Pelican Hotel does all the cream teas in Penwisk!' he said, banging his basket down on the wall.

Wimbleball padded over to an old cardboard box and jumped in. Turpin the tomcat was already in it, but Wimbleball didn't mind. He settled down to enjoy the argument.

'Ah, but Pelican Hotel cream teas are not the same as *my* cream teas,' said Miss Tripp, sweetly.

'A cream tea is a cream tea!' cried Henry. 'A pot of tea, two scones, strawberry jam and cream!'

'No it isn't!' said Miss Tripp. 'It's a pot of tea, two scones, strawberry jam and cream – and a chocolate twirly-whirly cake!'

A chocolate twirly-whirly cake! Wimbleball's eyes went as wide as gobstoppers. Turpin's ears stood up like sticks of rock. Quick as a flick they were out of the cardboard box, over the wall,

and in through the open door of Crab
Cottage.

And nobody noticed. Miss Tripp was too
busy feeling pleased with herself. Henry
was too busy wondering what a chocolate
twirly-whirly cake looked like. And Frank
was too busy hoping Miss Tripp had
forgotten about his smelly backyard.

He was also hoping that Henry knew a
good recipe for one crab, two tiddlers,
and a lump of seaweed.

Henry didn't, and went back to the
Pelican Hotel in a huff.

4 An Angry Neighbour

Crab Cottage didn't look a bit like Crab Cottage any more. Gone were the dusty floorboards, for a start. Turpin tried his claws out on the new pink carpet.

'Not bad,' he said.

Wimbleball padded under all the tables and chairs to his favourite corner. There was a big plant pot there now. He jumped up on to one of the tables and had a good look round. There were frilly tablecloths, frilly curtains, and frilly lampshades all over the place.

'No chocolate twirly-whirly cakes up here!' he said.

'None down here, either!' said Turpin, from behind a curtain.

Next they tried the kitchen.

The found lots of shiny teapots and lots of jars of jam. They found lots of scones under big glass tops. 'Goldfish bowls,' said Turpin. They found silver spoons and silver forks and piles of serviettes. But nothing that looked a bit like a chocolate twirly-whirly cake.

'Rats!' said Wimbleball.

They decided to have a game to cheer themselves up. The game was who could rip up the most serviettes.

'I won!' said Turpin.

'You must be joking!' said Wimbleball.

They decided afterwards it was all Miss Tripp's fault. It she hadn't left that jar of jam right on the edge of the table, it would never have fallen off when they had their fight about who'd ripped up the most serviettes.

But it did fall off, silly Miss Tripp, with a great big *thunk.* And then there was strawberry jam all over the place and Miss Tripp screeching in the doorway with a broom in her hand.

'Run for it!' hissed Wimbleball.

They darted for the doorway and got past Miss Tripp's broom by the skin of their teeth. Then Turpin ran straight home up Pansy Lane for his elevenses, and Wimbleball shot into his box in the kitchen of Kipper Cottage.

He could hear Miss Tripp going on and on outside.

'I want those horrible cats kept out of my tea-shop, Mr Fingle. If I ever find those horrible cats in my tea-shop again, I'll make mincemeat out of them! And don't just stand there, Mr Fingle! GET THAT SMELLY BACKYARD SORTED OUT!'

When he dared creep out of his box and peer round the kitchen door, Wimbleball got a shock. Frank had a bucket of hot soapy water and he was sploshing it all over the backyard and scrubbing it.

Wimbleball stayed where he was, safe and sound on the nice dry doormat, until Frank had finished. Then, when Frank sat down on his bench for a rest, he jumped up on his lap and settled down for a snooze.

No such luck.

'And what about all those nasty nets, Mr Fingle?' came the voice of Miss Tripp over the wall. 'And all that smelly old rubbish in the corner?'

'Smelly old rubbish?' said Frank. 'Those are my lobster pots and buckets, I'll have you know. And if your customers don't like them, they know what they can do about it!'

'What?' said Miss Tripp, her poky face getting pinker and pinker.

'Stick their noses in their chocolate twirly-whirly cakes!' said Frank. 'That's what!'

That night Wimbleball dreamed of chocolate twirly-whirly cakes. They were covered in cherries and cream and chocolate bits. And he ate six.

5 A Good Neighbour

The next day was the best fishing day
Frank and Wimbleball had ever had! Frank
was delighted.

'Wait till Miss Tripp smells this lot!'
he said.

But Miss Tripp didn't even notice. Miss
Tripp was sitting at a little table under a
bright yellow parasol, blowing her nose
and crying her eyes out.

'What's the matter?' asked Frank.

'The van hasn't come,' said Mrs Trundle,
importantly. Mrs Trundle was Miss Tripp's
new helper.

'What van?' asked Frank.

'The van from the bakery in Port Coddle,' said Mrs Trundle. 'It was bringing all the chocolate twirly-whirly cakes for opening day.'

Frank took his telescope out of his pocket and peered across the river. There it was. The van from the Port Coddle bakery. Stuck in a traffic jam on the Port Coddle road.

'It's all those holidaymakers,' he said. 'It'll be there for ages.'

'Rats!' went Wimbleball.

'I knew we should have made them ourselves!' sniffed Mrs Trundle.

'*Boo-hoo-hoo*!' went Miss Tripp. And off she rushed into Crab Cottage.

'Deary me!' beamed Frank. And off he went, whistling, to start unloading *Bobber*.

'Miaow!' mewed Wimbleball, suddenly. He'd had an idea.

'Oh what a beautiful MORNING!' sang Frank, pretending he hadn't noticed. 'Oh what a beautiful DAY! I've got a beautiful FEELING, EVERYTHING's going my way!'

'MIAOW!' howled Wimbleball crossly. Why didn't Frank want to hear about his idea?

Just then Mrs Trundle poked her head over the wall. 'Mr Fingle!' she cried. 'Miss Tripp has just had an idea!' But Frank had started on another song now:

'Oh, I DO like to be beside the seaside, oh, I DO like to be beside the sea! Oh, I DO like to stroll along the prom prom prom, where the brass band plays TIDDLY-OM-POM-POM!'

Frank and Wimbleball had pilchards for breakfast. Then Frank settled down to do the crossword. He was in a very good mood. Wimbleball wasn't.

Two minutes later there was a tap on the back door.

'Now I wonder who that can be?' said Frank, with a big grin on his face. 'Well I never! What a surprise!'

It was Miss Tripp. Miss Tripp with a blotchy face, a red nose, and a screwed-up hanky in her hand.

'Mr Fingle,' she said in a small voice. 'I've come to say something.'

'Something about my smelly backyard?' asked Frank.

'No,' said Miss Tripp.

'Something about my horrible cat?' asked Frank.

'No' said Miss Tripp, her voice getting smaller and smaller.

'Something about your chocolate twirly-whirly cakes?'

'Yes,' whispered Miss Tripp. 'I was wondering if you could fetch them for me in your boat, Mr Fingle! Please!'

'Miaow!' went Wimbleball, shooting off between Miss Tripp's legs with his tail in the air.

'Well now,' said Frank, scratching his beard. 'The thing is, Miss Tripp, I'm a fisherman, and proud of it. And we fishermen use our boats for fishing, not for rescuing sticky buns from traffic jams.'

Miss Tripp closed her eyes and screwed up her hanky even tighter.

'I came to say something else as well, Mr Fingle.'

'And what was that, Miss Tripp?'

'I've been very nasty and very horrible and I'm very, very sorry!'

In no time at all Frank and Wimbleball were tying up at the other side of the River Wisk. The man from the bakery unloaded all the chocolate twirly-whirly cakes from his van. Frank loaded them all into *Bobber*.

They were covered in cherries and cream and chocolate bits – and Wimbleball wasn't allowed to touch a single one.

Then back across the river they came, bringing not only all the chocolate twirly-whirly cakes, but Miss Tripp's very first customers as well. They were holidaymakers, fed up with being stuck in the traffic jam.

All that day Miss Tripp and Mrs Trundle were rushed off their feet. The tea-shop was so busy that there was a queue. Miss Tripp told everyone that the Pelican Hotel served nice teas, too, so some people went there instead.

That made Henry happy, because he'd been up half the night, making buns. Banana crunchy-wunchy buns, he called them.

At tea-time Miss Tripp came round to Kipper Cottage to say thank you.
She brought with her a tray with a pot of

tea, two scones, strawberry jam and cream
— and a pile of chocolate twirly-whirly
cakes!

'My first name's Tabitha, by the way,'
she said with a blush. And off she went
without saying a single word about Frank's
smelly backyard. And the funny thing was,
all the customers liked Frank's smelly
backyard. They said it was a real
fisherman's backyard. It really made them
feel on holiday. Someone even asked if
Frank did round trips in his boat.

'I might,' said Frank.

Frank gave Wimbleball a chocolate
twirly-whirly cake to try. Wimbleball ate
half of it and saved the other half for
Turpin. It tasted very nice. Very nice
indeed. But not half as nice as some things
he could think of.

In the middle of the night a terrible scream
came from Crab Cottage. The mice were

still there, you see, having a fine time with all the crumbs from the tea-shop.

And Miss Tabitha Tripp hated mice.

In fact, standing there on a chair in her nightie, she decided that she hated mice even more than she hated cats.

After a while Wimbleball wandered
round to Crab Cottage to see if the crack
at the top of the kitchen window was there.
And guess what. It was.